W9-DBZ-344

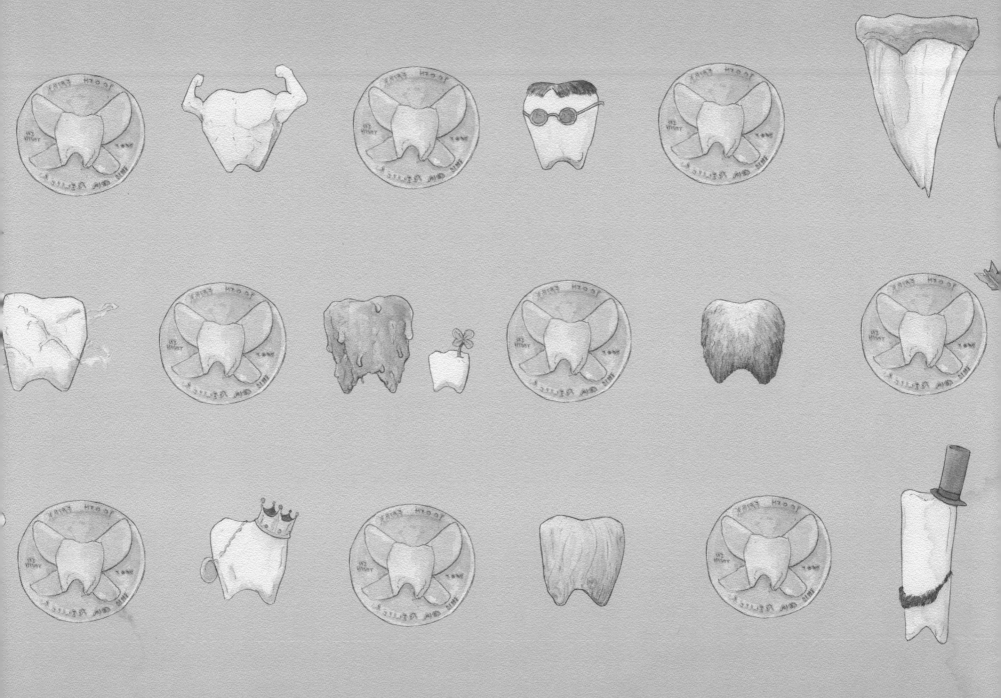

Mary the Tooth Fairy

Written and Illustrated by Nick Bell

red
cygnet®
PRESS

San Diego, California

red cygnet® PRESS

I would like to dedicate this book to my sister Jess, who asked one question that started Mary's crazy journey. "How does the Tooth Fairy get around?" I hope I answered her question and any others she might have had about the Tooth Fairy.–N.B.

Illustrations copyright © 2008 Nick Bell
Manuscript copyright © 2008 Nick Bell
Book copyright © 2008 Red Cygnet Press, Inc., 11858 Stoney Peak Dr. #525, San Diego, CA 92128

All rights reserved. No part of this book may be reproduced or transmitted in any form or by any means whatsoever without prior written permission of the publisher.

Cover and book design: Amy Stirnkorb

First Edition 2008
10 9 8 7 6 5 4 3 2
Printed in China

Library of Congress Cataloging-in-Publication Data

Bell, Nick.
  Mary the Tooth Fairy / written and illustrated by Nick Bell. -- 1st ed.
      p. cm.
  Summary: When the old Tooth Fairy slows down and almost gets caught a few times, she trains Mary, who proves to be a natural, to take her place delivering coins to children who have lost teeth.
  ISBN 978-1-60108-015-8
  [1. Tooth fairy--Fiction. 2. Fairies--Fiction.] I. Title.
  PZ7.B41159Mar 2007
  [E]--dc22
2006036763

"Well, well, well. What do we have here?" Mr. Stork said, as he stumbled past a recently hatched egg in his delivery room. "Very strange. You are the first babe from a Christmas egg ever to hatch with wings."

Still bewildered, Mr. Stork bundled up the little babe and set off to deliver her to Santa's workshop.

The loud knock on the workshop door startled the elves. When Santa answered, he was surprised to see Mr. Stork. A visit from Mr. Stork was always a joyful occasion, of course, but Santa was not expecting any deliveries.

"I'm not sure why this one has wings, but she hatched out of a Christmas egg and you know the rules. All newborn babes that hatch out of Christmas eggs get delivered here."

Santa was as confused as Mr. Stork, but the jolly old man was not one to turn away a present.

The elves all crowded 'round. "What are you going to name her?" one elf asked.

"How about Mary?" another elf shouted. "She's got wings like a fairy. And Mary rhymes with fairy."

Santa bellowed a big belly laugh. "I like that!" he said. "I like that very much!"

From the moment she arrived, Mary was an annoyance to the elves. She couldn't keep her hands off the shiny gadgets around the workshop.

No matter where she was put, she would reach out and grab the nearest shiny thing.

As she grew, Mary's wings became a big problem. Her ability to dart quickly from place to place made it impossible for the elves to keep an eye on her.

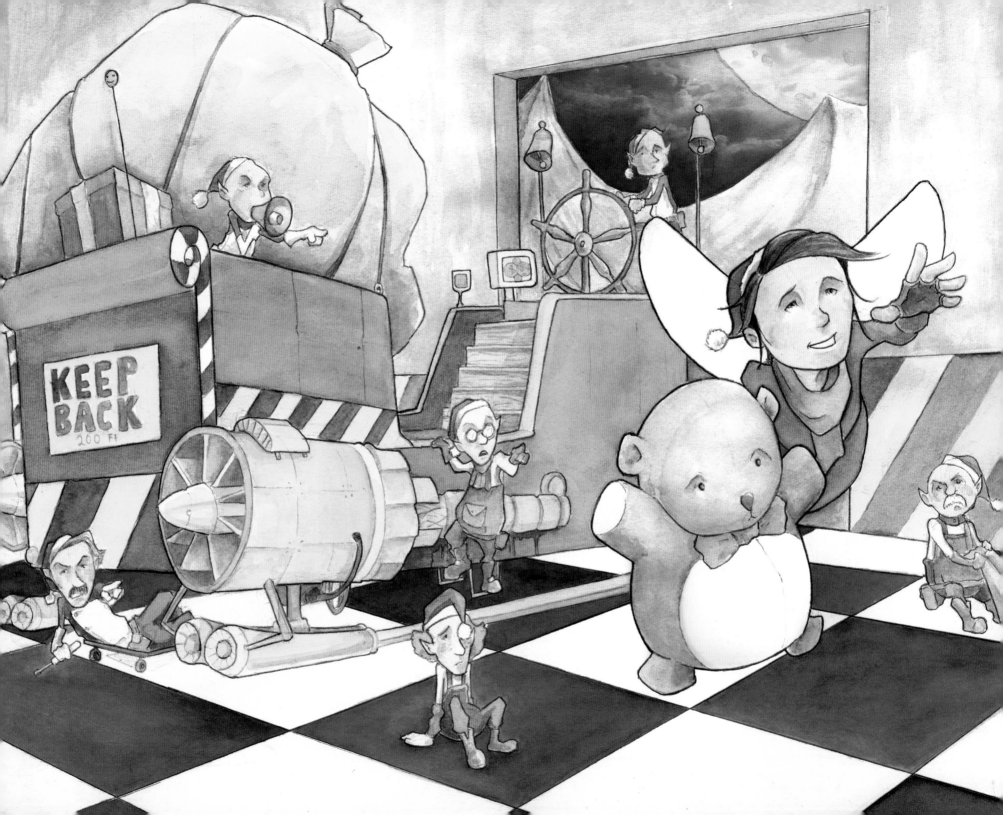

As Mary got older, the elves scolded her constantly. "Mary, keep your hands off the toys!" they demanded. But Mary could not stop herself. In fact, she became so good at snatching spinning tops, little red tricycles, and jingle bells that the elves could never get an accurate count of how many toys they had actually made!

The elves complained constantly to Santa.

Santa agreed that something had to be done. As he often does when he has a problem, Santa called Mother Goose.

Mother Goose could hear that Santa was upset when he called. "I love Mary like she was my own, but I fear she does not belong in my workshop," Santa explained. Mother Goose replied, "I know just the place for one with such talents."

Mother Goose rang the Tooth Fairy and told her about Mary's amazing flying and snatching abilities. "Send her up, right away!" the Tooth Fairy squealed. She was overjoyed. She needed some extra help around her castle. She was getting very old, very slow, and very clumsy. In fact, she had almost been seen three times in the past month, after waking sleeping children while she was under their pillows.

"But I don't want to leave." Mary said as she hugged Santa for the last time. "I have loved you like one of my own, Mary," Santa said with a tear in his eye. "But your special skills are needed elsewhere."

"Come now, we mustn't be late," Mother Goose chirped. "You are expected at the Tooth Fairy's castle any moment now." Mother Goose helped Mary load her belongings into the Goose-mobile. Within seconds, they shot off — straight into the atmosphere.

"Wow!" Mary said, as she stood in front of the Tooth Fairy's gleaming castle. "This place is huge. I hope I can find her." Nervous and a little scared, Mary grabbed her things and went inside.

The first room Mary entered was called the Hall of Teeth. "Hello? Anyone here?" Mary shouted. But all she heard was her echo. As Mary looked around, she became mesmerized by all the shiny teeth.

Mary leaned in closer to admire one of the shiniest teeth in the hall. As she stared, a voice startled her.

"Hello!" squeaked the Tooth Fairy. She had snuck up on Mary without her noticing. "How did you do that?" Mary asked.

"Why, I'm the Tooth Fairy! And with the proper training, you will be able to sneak into and out of just about anywhere unnoticed — just like me."

"Would you like a shot at becoming the new Tooth Fairy?" the Tooth Fairy asked. Mary was puzzled. The Tooth Fairy continued: "I am getting old and slow and have almost been caught three times. You know what that means, don't you?" "Why, no," Mary answered quietly.

"If I get seen, I'm gone! That's it! Kapoof! No more Tooth Fairy! And toothless children forever more will have nothing under their pillows in the morning."

Mary was saddened and worried by the sound of that. She decided she couldn't resist a chance to become the new Tooth Fairy. So, Mary agreed.

Mary began her training right away. It took months. On her trial runs, she was quite a natural at getting under pillows and replacing teeth with coins. The super-sensitive motion sensors on the practice robots never even went off.

The only thing Mary did better than sneaking was flying. Her flying abilities were better than the Tooth Fairy's had been at Mary's age.

The one skill Mary did need to work at was her self-control. Every day, she became better and better at only taking the few metal practice coins she needed for that day. It was difficult for her to leave all the other shiny coins in the practice pile! But Mary soon learned to control her desire.

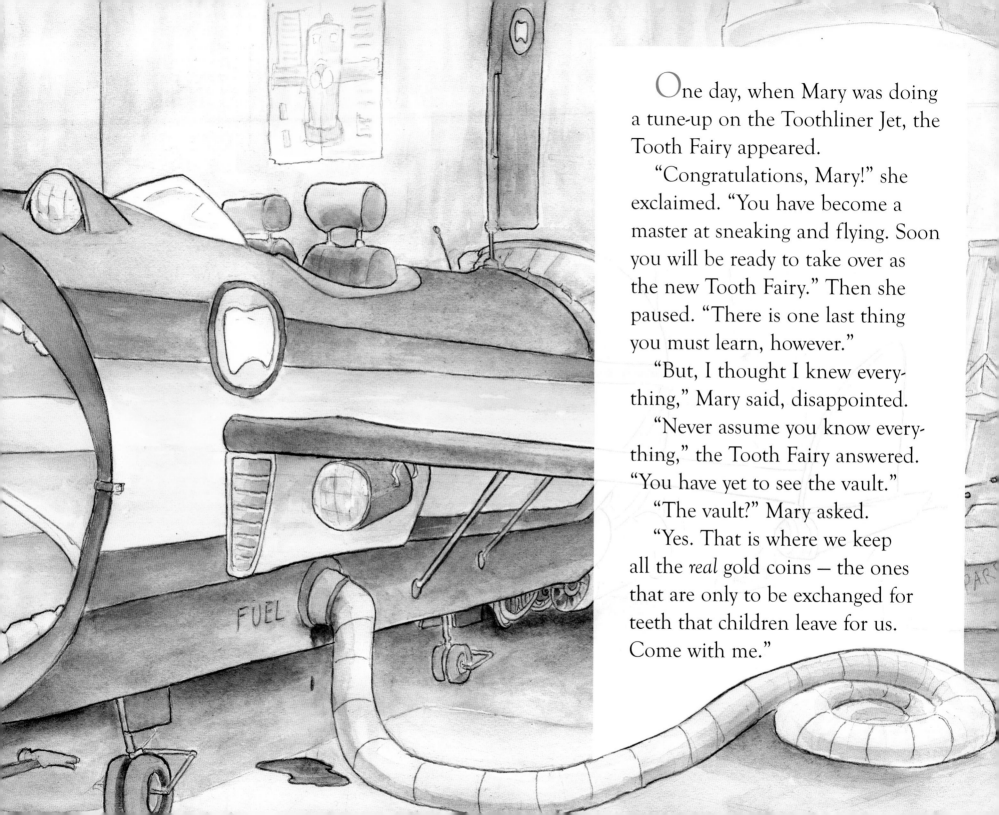

One day, when Mary was doing a tune-up on the Toothliner Jet, the Tooth Fairy appeared.

"Congratulations, Mary!" she exclaimed. "You have become a master at sneaking and flying. Soon you will be ready to take over as the new Tooth Fairy." Then she paused. "There is one last thing you must learn, however."

"But, I thought I knew everything," Mary said, disappointed.

"Never assume you know everything," the Tooth Fairy answered. "You have yet to see the vault."

"The vault?" Mary asked.

"Yes. That is where we keep all the *real* gold coins — the ones that are only to be exchanged for teeth that children leave for us. Come with me."

"Do you know why we keep the coins locked up?" the Tooth Fairy asked. "It's because of the Sandman." The Tooth Fairy shivered as she spoke his name.

"He has been after my coins and my magic sack for as long as I have been the Tooth Fairy. You need to avoid him at all costs. The magic sack can hold all the teeth and coins you could ever dream of. If he gets his sandy little hands on it, there will be no way to bring joy to all the children who are expecting coins for their teeth."

A few weeks later, the Tooth Fairy went out on a routine run collecting molars.

She had been gone longer than usual when Mary got an emergency call on the alert screen. The Tooth Fairy looked very upset.

"Oh, Mary. It's terrible! It finally happened!" the Tooth Fairy cried. "I was too slow and the Sandman nabbed me."

"What can I do?" Mary asked with courage in her voice.

"He has the magic sack and is asking for you. You must come at once! You are my only chance." Without another thought, Mary took flight and was off.

When Mary arrived on the scene, she saw that the Sandman had tied up the Tooth Fairy with a roll of unwaxed dental floss. And he had the magic sack!

"You better let her go!" Mary shouted.

"Now why would I do a thing like that?" the Sandman said with a grin. "Consider this, Mary: You and I could keep this sack of shiny, shiny coins and never leave any more for anyone else! Just imagine it. No coins for the children and you'd never have to answer to anyone."

Mary's face turned red with anger. She shouted back. "You can't do that! We need to bring happiness to those children! If I side with you, all my hard work and training would have been for nothing! I won't let that happen! Now free the Tooth Fairy and return the sack or else!"

The Sandman stood frozen. There was silence.

"Congratulations, my dear!" the Tooth Fairy shouted out. "You have passed the final test."

"But the Sandman! You told me —"

"Calm down Mary," the Tooth Fairy said, as the Sandman untied her. "The Sandman was never a threat. We have actually been friends for quite some time now. In fact, we are planning to retire together."

Mary was stunned.

"Don't you see?" the Tooth Fairy went on. "You passed the final test! You overcame your biggest weakness and resisted temptation." Congratulations! You will be the new Tooth Fairy!"

"Many great adventures lie ahead of you, Mary," the Tooth Fairy said, as they flew back to the castle. "I hope you are ready. There are a lot of teeth down there that need to be collected!"

Mary smiled a big smile. "I am more than ready!" she replied. "And I can't wait to get started. I feel like I was born to do this." Mary leaned in and gave the Tooth Fairy a big hug.

Everyone who was anyone was at Mary's official celebration. "Look at our Mary, all grown up," Santa said, as tears rolled down his cheeks. The Tooth Fairy placed the keys to the castle around Mary's neck. "You are officially the new Tooth Fairy. Now all this is yours. Trust in your beliefs and always bring joy to the children." The crowd cheered. Mary blushed as she swelled with pride.

After the crowd had left, Mary cleaned and polished up the castle. When she was done, she loaded her plane with coins and took to the air. It was going to be her very first night as the new Tooth Fairy. As she headed toward her first stop, she couldn't help but smile. She was finally doing the one thing she was truly born to do.

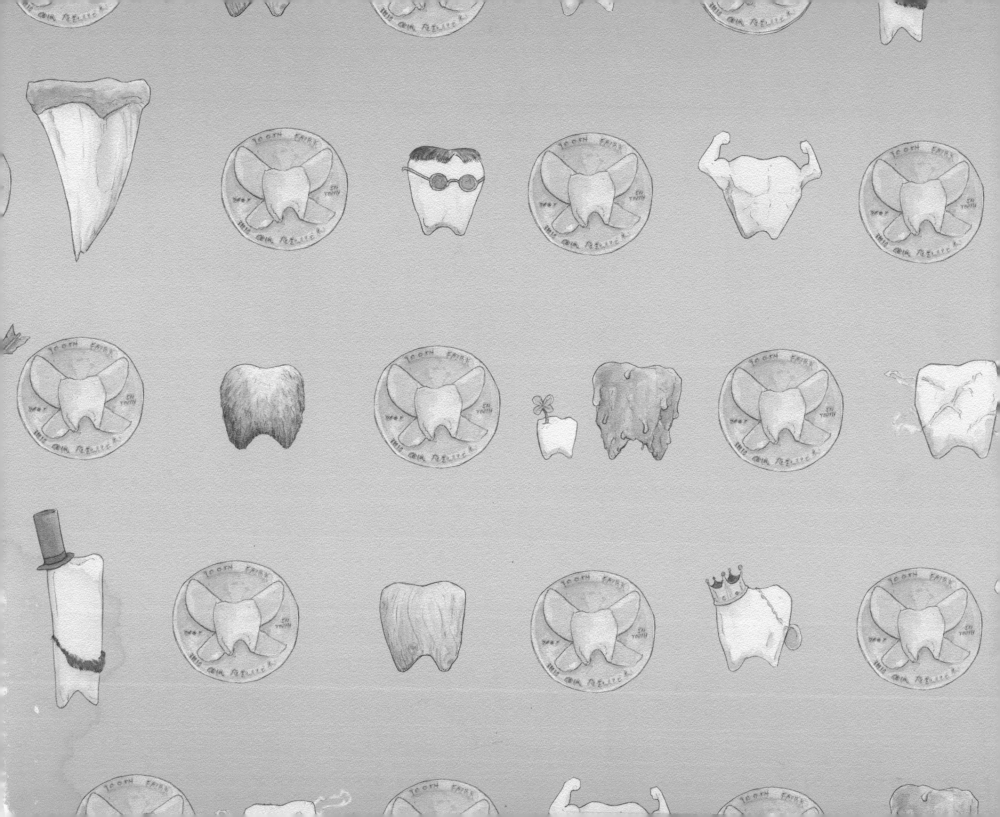